I0538314

Dedication:

To all the people who have ever been in a relationship because you wanted to save face. You can't help what the Heart wants. Let your heart guide you. Be in a relationship because you "W*ant to be*", not because you *"Have to be"*

"Sometimes the heart sees what is invisible to the eye."
S. Jackson Brown, Jr.

Special Thank you

Jason Kercheski or "Jason Jc Kurtis" as some of you know him. Thank you for always answering any questions I have regarding the military. You will always be my #1 Military Advisor in any book that I write. ***"Don't H8te Motiv8te"***

#TeamResilience

All rights reserved, including the right to reproduce this book, or portions thereof, in any form without written permission except for the brief quotations embodied in critical articles and reviews.

This work is a work of fiction. Names, characters, places, and incidents either are a product of the author's imagination or are used factiously, and any resemblance to actual persons, living or dead, business establishments, events or locales is entirely coincidental. Confidentiality Notice: This e-mail message, including any attachments, is for the sole use of the intended recipient(s), and may contain legally privileged and confidential information. Any unauthorized review, use, disclosure, or distribution is prohibited. If you are not the intended recipient, please do not read, copy, or use it, and do not disclose it to others. Please notify the sender of the delivery error by replying to this message, then delete it from your system, and destroy all copies. Thank you.

Layla Stevens is not responsible for broken E-readers, Kindles, Nooks, and or Phones due to you throwing them.

Copyright © 2016 Layla Stevens

What the Heart Wants

Published by:

The Scilicet Group, LLC
4139 South Nolan Drive
Pearland, Texas 77584
281-489-1113
Thescilicetgroup.com

ISBN-13:
978-1-941839-15-7

Chapter One

"Distance between two hearts is not an obstacle...rather a beautiful reminder of just how strong true love can be." ~ Author Unknown

"Here let me help you with that!" my wife Grace said as she came up behind me. "You're all thumbs, tonight. Your mom and dad would be very proud of you. I know I am!" She continued saying while she buttoned the last button on my jacket and double checked my pins. "I'm sure they're in heaven givin' the angels hell, but I know for sure they're smiling down tonight."

I wipe a single tear, that's escaped my ocean blue eyes.

"Thanks honey!" I said softly. Knowing tonight was not just going to be long, but a little stressful as well. I just hoped that I did my parents proud and that a certain corporal would also be there.

"My wayward thoughts of him make my dick twitch with anticipation. I know Trevor will be here tonight; and tonight, I will tell him everything--how I feel, how long I've wanted him, and the entire contents of my soul. I refuse to hide who I am any longer-- DADT be damned. (DADT is Don't ask, don't tell). I simply can't deny my heart any longer. He owns my heart, and tonight, I want to own his body"

My wife interrupted my thoughts. "I'm all set. You ready?"

"Yep, let's go!" I turned and saw my wife. She was in a stunning, red, floor length low-cut evening gown. "You look beautiful!" I quickly said, kissed the side of her cheek and opened the door for her.

I see the longing in her emerald green eyes, I know she wants more from me, but I just can't give her something that I don't have. We married because it was the right thing to do. I was young and fresh out of boot camp, and I was looking to get away, and I ran into her. She was beautiful even back then with her medium brown hair with blonde highlights, but what caught my attention was the man standing beside her. But in the military that is something that is not done. Two men are not together, E-V-E-R! So I did the gentleman like thing and I ignored the handsome man standing beside her and I asked her out. I knew who she was, hell the whole damn state of Virginia, knew who she was. She came from money and several of my comrades have tried to as they say 'tap that' but she always turned them down.

Grace must have seen something in me because I took her home that day. We got married soon after, and everyone thinks that we have a marriage made in heaven; but actually, its hell. It wasn't so bad when I was overseas on tours. However, when I came home from the second tour, we really began to struggle.

When I was away, life was easy, plain, and simple. Did I miss being home? Yes, of course, but I didn't want to be home with *her*. I want a home with someone who completes me, someone who makes my knees weak, and Grace is not that person.

She never has been.

Chapter Two

"If you can't get them to salute when they should salute and wear the clothes you tell them to wear, how are you going to get them to die for their country?" — *George Patton*

We rode in silence the entire way there. My thoughts are not on this speech. My thoughts are not even on Grace. I know that I should be a bundle of nerves, because I'm about to destroy my marriage. For what? I don't even know if he feels the same way, but I can't live in a loveless marriage any longer.

Grace knew I was worried about this evening's events, but deep down she knew something else was bothering me. She just couldn't quite put her finger on it. I know there will be questions later.

My mind was full of tonight's events, but more so, it was filled with a certain corporal. Cpl. Tavington, aka Trevor, was the source of all synaptical activity. From the moment Trevor was transferred to my platoon, I was hooked. There was no doubt it was Trevor's eyes and shyness that drew me to him.

Pulling into my vehicle into City Hall, I parked instead of using the valet. As Grace interlocked arms with me, I knew at one point in our marriage I had loved her but what my heart truly wanted was not her. I know she felt me flinch, she grabbed my arm tighter.

I couldn't be happy in a relationship, let alone a marriage if I wasn't happy with myself. One person has captured my soul. I want to be able to scream to the top of the world how much he means to me but tonight I'll just whisper in his ear you are my world. Tonight Trevor will know, and so will Grace. I know she will not take this lying down, she will make this difficult. When she finds out I'm leaving her she will be pissed, but that I'm leaving her for a man, she will try her best to nail my balls to the wall.

Just outside the door, Grace couldn't hold it in any longer, "Honey, you seem on edge. What's bothering you?"

"I'm sorry, I guess tonight's event is weighing heavy. I just don't want to screw it up."

"You'll do fine, Sarge!"

Spinning around, there stood a strapping young man. Clean cut, blonde hair and those baby blues. I'd know his body anywhere. It's him, and my knees almost buckle.

"My apologies, ma'am. Good evening, Sarge."

"Grace, this is Cpl. Tavington." My heart raced as I made the introduction.

Extending his hand, Cpl. Tavington replied, "Please call me Trevor, and it's an honor, ma'am."

With that said, Trevor held the door for Grace and me.

"Thank you Cpl." I acknowledged, walking by Trevor. I could smell the aftershave he was wearing. It heightened my senses, and my manhood jostled in my boxers, making my trousers strained and walking almost uncomfortable.

The center of the room was literally packed with fellow soldiers and officers with their families. All Army personnel were dressed in their Class A's and the women were in full length, red evening gowns. This was going to be a spectacular night to honor and raise money for the American Heart Foundation--a foundation which is very close to my own heart.

Looking around I found our table. Leading Grace to where we are to sit, I then pulled her chair out and asked, "Something to drink?"

"Please honey. Sweet tea is fine." She replied, as she started mingling with the other women at the table.

Making my way to the bar, I tried to acknowledge all the waves and hands shakes, but I hadn't seen the one person I really wanted to since we had arrived.

"What can I get you?" The bartender asked.

"Sweet tea and a bud light in a bottle."

"Are you following me, Sarge?"

Turning towards the voice, I saw Trevor. Without saying anything, I quickly scribbled on the napkin in front of me and handed it to Trevor. The bartender then returned with my drinks, and within seconds, I was back at the table.

"Here you go babe!" I placed Grace's glass in front of her. When she saw I had a beer, she eyeballed me but didn't say anything. This wasn't the time or the place.

Sitting next to my wife, I tried to converse with the other men but my mind was completely on Trevor and the note I had just slipped him. Glancing at my watch, 6:20 p.m., dinner wouldn't be served for another forty minutes.

"Excuse me." I interrupted my wife as she was speaking to another woman. "I'm going to get some air."

"Okay hun."

I replied with a small kiss to the top of her head and quickly made my way to the door.

Chapter Three

"Bravery is being the only one who knows you're afraid." —David Hackworth Li

Three buildings down and into the dark alley, I just hoped Trevor had read the napkin. Turning the corner, there stood Trevor. Not only was my heart racing, but there was an aching throb in my Class A's.

"Hey Sarge! What's up? Why did you want to meet all the way over here?" Trevor was really hoping it was for a quick fuck, but he didn't want to cross the boundaries of ethics or friendship.

Walking straight to him, I was blunt, "For one, don't look at the uniform. Two, I wanted privacy and I wouldn't get it in there. Three, I'm going to fuck you right here, right now!"

Trevor didn't have time to react; I had crushed Trevor's lips with mine. Forcing my tongue in, dancing it around as my hands groped the front of Trevor's trousers.

Grunting, Trevor felt his tool pushing against the fabric into Anthony's hand.

Pulling away, I said, "Drop em!"

His eyes not once leaving mine, Trevor unfastened his pants.

Feeling his own pulse wanting release, I said, "Turn around!"

As Trevor turned, he heard the sound of foil being torn and Anthony moaning slightly as he rolled the cover over himself.

Placing one hand on the base of myself and the other on Trevor's lower back, I then spread Trevor's legs with my feet.

Bracing himself on the wall, Trevor waited in anticipation to feel Anthony in him. He knew any second his mentor would invade him as no man ever had.

Knowing he didn't have much time, I placed my latex covered mushroom at Trevor's entrance. Feeling Trevor's tightness he said, "Relax, just relax."

Trevor relaxed as much as he could as I began to push upward. Once I was able to begin a steady pace, I held onto both Trevor's hips and buried even deeper.

Handling himself at Anthony's pace, Trevor knew it wouldn't be long before he would explode.

Both men quietly moaned as they were reaching their peak.

Just as I stiffened my body and filled the latex, Trevor sprayed the brick wall in front of him.

"Oh fuck!" I exhaled as I pulled out of Trevor.

Shaking the rest of his cream off, Trevor turned around. Both men facing one another, their still stiffness lying against one another.

As I reached down to help Trevor pull his pants back up, I flicked my tongue forcefully across Trevor's mushroom head. "Oh Sarge. Fuck!"

As we both adjusted the other's uniform, I said, "Thank you CPL, when the ball is over, I want you to meet me at the Country Inn, room #225. This time it won't be just a fast fuck. Now if you will excuse me I have to get back to my wife and prepare for my speech."

Chapter Four

"To the soldier, luck is merely another word for skill."
Patrick MacGill

Trevor was left standing in the dark alley, literally speechless. After collecting his thoughts, he too made his way back to the City Hall.

Back at the table, Grace asked, "Everything okay?"

"Yes, everything's fine. I just needed air and to relieve myself."

If she only knew what kind of release to which I was referring.

The two of us sat in silence until the waiters began to bring their plates. There was then only small talk.

Dinner wasn't half bad. I had eaten my entire meal and asked for a second plate. I hadn't eaten like this in a while. It has also been a long time since I had a good fuck too.

Yes, I force myself to have sex with Grace, but having sex with her and having sex with Trevor was like night and day. With Grace, I tried my best to rush things, but damn with Trevor I busted my load and I just left him. How selfish of me. Tonight, if he shows I'll worship him, I'll show him that it's him owns my heart. I look up at Grace.

"Glad to see you eating!" Grace whispered, leaning in.

"I feel pretty good." I replied.

"Sure you are, with all that alcohol in your system." She said, glaring at me.

If she only knew what brought my appetite on.

"Do you have something you want to say Grace?" I whisper.

"You reek of some cheap whore. I know she's in here somewhere."

"Grace, stop. I will not have you embarrass me or any of the officers and their families because you are being a brat."

I see the anger in her face, but I know I have made my point because she will not do anything that will tarnish her reputation.

I grab my beer and take a swig, and she gives me a *'go fuck you'* look.

Within the next thirty minutes, the tables were cleared except for drinks. It was now time to start the speeches.

My speech wasn't until near the end. So, I ended up waving down a waiter to bring me another beer. Despite the looks my wife was giving right now, I drank up.

The other speakers went by fairly quickly. Grace nudged me letting me know it was my turn to go up. Unlike earlier in the evening, I was now confident and ready. The audience applauded as I made my way to center stage. Once the applauding came to a cease, I skimmed the room for Trevor. A feeling of gratification overcame me and I began:

My fellow comrades, families and distinguished guest, it is an honor and a privilege to be speaking here tonight, in honor of the American Heart Foundation. As many of you know, I lost both of my parents Gen. Tim LaRouse and Cpt. Annette LaRouse to this horrible disease. It's called the 'silent killer' because most symptoms go unnoticed. 1 in every 4 Americans die each year from some sort of heart condition. That's roughly 610,000 people every year. With your donations, more research can be done to help decrease these numbers. Amongst you are heart shaped bowls, I

ask not only for myself but for all the families, please donate what you can. Every little bit helps. In closing I would like to thank my wife, Grace for her continued support for the past 17 years. Thank you all for coming and enjoy the rest of your evening.

My eyes not once left Trevor's, not even when I acknowledged my wife. The only thing that consumed my mind was meeting Trevor in a short couple of hours.

As I made I exit, I shook hands with most of the officers and then joined my wife back at our table. I sat in silence as the ceremony ended and the dance began. Not being much of a dancer, I just sat back and watched as my wife enjoyed herself.

Chapter Five

"A soldier will fight long and hard for a bit of colored ribbon."
Napoleon Bonaparte

"Good speech, Sarge!"

I knew who it was without turning, nodding my head in gesture for Trevor to sit. "Thanks Cpl."

"Sarge, earlier I don't . . . "

I cut him short, "Not here Cpl. Now if you will excuse me, I need to go amuse my wife." I excused myself from Trevor's company even though the only thing I wanted to do was take Trevor in my arms and show him real passion.

Making my way to the dance floor, I embraced my wife under false pretenses, dancing to Kenny G., *The Moment.*

Tonight would be the night I tell her it was over.

As the song came to an end, Grace whispered, "I'm proud of you honey. Your parents would be very proud of you, too!"

"Thanks." I replied, kissing her forehead.

"I'm sorry about earlier. Tony, I know you'd never cheat on me. I'm sure it was because you hugged a woman too closely. Right?"

I didn't answer just looked at her. I know she knows something is up. She's not a stupid woman.

Walking back to their table, Grace spoke up, "Do you think it would be okay to leave a bit early?"

"Is this another one of your headaches, Grace?" I asked.

"Honey, I'm sorry. I don't mean to spoil your evening."

I agreed to take her home. After excusing ourselves, we made our way through the crowd to the front door.

Once on our way, Grace again apologized and in the same breath she tried to kiss ass by commending me on my speech.

I heard what she said but I really wasn't listening. My mind was on Trevor. How I wanted to bed him properly.

Pulling in the driveway, Grace got out and asked, "Aren't you coming in?"

"No, I'm going back for a little while. Don't wait up." I replied, continuously staring out the windshield.

"Okay. Please be careful. I love you."

"I will. Love you too!"

I don't know why I just lied to her. I don't love her. In the years we've been together, I don't think I've truly loved her, not like she needed to be loved. Grace is a good woman, but I know I'm not who she needs. She needs a man who will love her for her, and a man who will give her what she wants. One of the many things I never gave her over the years was that love and adoration she truly deserved. Grace deserves better than what I can offer her. A loveless marriage is not what I want any longer.

She has asked me for years to have children. I have always told her that I didn't want to bring children into the world when I wouldn't be there to help raise them. Truth of the matter is, I never wanted children with her. I want children someday, but I want to adopt. I don't want biological children. There are too many children out there than need loving families. When I was overseas, there were always children with no parents, and my heart would break because they had no one to look out for them.

As soon as she shut the door, I was backing out of the driveway. Driving straight to the Inn, I knew the ball would be over shortly, and I held onto anticipation as to whether Trevor would show.

Getting in the room, flipping the light on, no wonder it was so cheap. "I guess you get what you pay for!" I said out loud.

There was a full size bed, old box TV on a lengthy dresser, table with two chairs in one corner of the room, and a sink offset the bathroom on the other side of the room.

"FUCK!" I yelled. The one thing I wanted to make sure I had, I was out. I had forgotten covers. If Trevor didn't have any, I would have to go bareback. I had never gone bareback, not even with Grace. I'd always made sure there was never an accidental pregnancy.

In that instant, the door knob turned and my heart began beating fast and the palms of my hands were sweaty. I hadn't been this nervous, hell, I hadn't ever been this nervous.

Coming in, Trevor shut and locked the door, now standing in front of me. For the first few minutes the two just stared into one another's eyes.

Chapter Six

"I wonder if a soldier ever does mend a bullet hole in his coat."
Clara Barton

Trevor broke the silence by saying, "You gave a good speech tonight, Sarge. Your parents would be damn proud."

"Thanks. I appreciate that, but I don't want to talk about that right now. What I want to do doesn't involve talking, well, not much anyway."

Leaning down a bit, my lips met Trevor's. Genuine, gentle, and meant to be. Forcing my tongue inside Trevor's mouth, our breathing hastened. Feeling my junk pressing against my Class A's, I took a step back. I didn't want to rush this, like the alley way. I want to take my time and savor every inch of Trevor's body.

As Trevor reached up to unbutton his jacket, I stopped him, "Here, let me!"

Trevor lowered his arms as I slowly undressed him. Tossing his clothes in a pile across the room, standing back, I simply admired this handsome man standing in front of me. Stepping forward, it was Trevor's turn to undress me. He slowly removed every article of clothing from my aching body.

When our lips met this time, it was with fierce passion. Our hands began to explore one another's body as our tongues danced in each other's mouth.

I didn't have to say anything verbally; my rising tool said it all. Trevor gently pushed me down on the bed. Scooting to the middle,

I lay flat on my back as Trevor climbed on the bed beside me grasping my thickness, squeezing and stroking.

I let out a groan feeling Trevor manhandling my goods.

"Hey Sarge, I think you have a growing problem here," Trevor said, pumping a little faster.

"Care to help with that problem, Cpl.?" I replied, exhaling.

"Is that an order?"

"Trevor, it's a request, please," I said, lifting my hips up a bit, practically begging.

Leaning down, Trevor ran his tongue the length of my thick pole.

"Sss….ahh!" I let out.

Covering his mouth over my mushroomed head, Trevor slowly lowered, consuming my entire shaft in his mouth. Rolling his tongue around in circular motion, I reached down grabbing what little hair Trevor had on his head.

Coming back up, Trevor then went back down making slurping sounds the whole way. While Trevor sucked the hell out of my cock, I reached with my other hand for Trevor, gripping and stroking with the same rhythm as Trevor's mouth.

We both groaned, feeling the other growing and thickening even more.

As Trevor came up and off me, he asked, "Cover?"

Shaking his head no, I then replied, "I know you're clean, and I'm clean. We can go bareback. I want you on all fours."

As Trevor got on all fours, I crawled in behind him on my knees. Trevor's ass was even muscular; I gave it a good, hard slap. Not expecting it, Trevor jumped a bit and let out a groan of excitement.

Holding the base of my shaft, I rubbed the tip of my head across Trevor's starfish hole. Leaning down I grasped Trevor's pole.

"Fuck!" Trevor yelled out, feeling me pushing in, breaking his barrier.

Inch by inch, I invaded his darkness and at the same time kept Trevor hard and ready with his soft yet masculine hands.

Once fully in, I let go of Trevor's pole and held onto his hips. My rhythm became fast and hard. Grunting as a feeling of completeness overwhelmed me. There was no other feeling as this and one that I had never felt, even with my wife.

Sweat pouring off my face, I wanted to finish but I waited for Trevor to give a sign that he was also ready.

Both our grunts and moans became loud and our breathing was labored.

Chapter Seven

"No one hates war like a soldier hates war." Tommy Franks

"Jesus, fuck, yes Sarge!" Trevor let out.

That was my sign to let loose, and I did. Pumping a few more times, I stiffened my body and sprayed the inside of Trevor's dark hole with hot cream.

Feeling this, Trevor said, "Swallow me, Sarge."

I quickly pulled out and Trevor, and laid flat on my back. Wrapping my lips tightly around Trevor's pole, I slid down quickly and then back up.

Only doing this a few times, Trevor unleashed a fiery of seed down my throat. Swallowing every bit, I then licked and sucked Trevor dry.

Both out of breath and very satisfied, we now lay in one another's arms just holding each other.

After a few minutes, Trevor asked, "Sarge, are you going to tell your wife?"

Turning around facing Trevor, I gently kissed him and said, "I will tell her I want a divorce. If she asks me anything, I won't lie. You know as much as I do, we can't be kicked out for being gay."

Trevor closed his eyes and I, at that moment, realized the truth about myself. I was gay.

Once Trevor was sound asleep, I slipped out of bed, dressed, and headed home.

Pulling in the driveway, I glanced at the clock on the dash. It was now 2:17 a.m. Grace would surely be asleep.

Quietly going inside, I took my uniform off and slipped into bed. Grace was not asleep and she asked, "Who is she, Anthony?"

I didn't reply at first, but when Grace moved closer to him in the bed I said, "Grace, I want a divorce!"

"Excuse me? You want a what?"

"You heard me Grace. I'm not happy. Hell, I've never been happy. I married you because it was the proper thing to do."

"Tony, what are you talking about? Proper thing to do? We dated for two years? Why wouldn't we get married?"

"Grace, do you really want me say it, or are you just going to accept that I want a divorce and leave it at that?

"N-O-! I will not leave it at that. I want to know who the home wrecking whore is. You tell me now, Tony. I have a right to know."

"First off, let me stop you right there. He is no whore. I love him, and I will be with him.

"You are fucking a man? Have you lost your god-dammned mind?"

"Grace, I'm sorry you had to find out like this. I wish there was an easier way for me to say it, but I never loved you. You wondered why we never had children. It's because I'm gay. I've denied it for years, but I'm tired of hiding my true feelings, and I will no longer hide my love for Trevor."

"Trevor, from tonight? You fucked him tonight didn't you?"

"I did and guess what? Then I came back and kissed you and the forehead."

I got out of the bed, dressed, and pack a couple bags. I reflected for a moment on the seriousness of the situation as I drew a deep breath, and then said, "I will get the rest of my things tomorrow and will be filing for a divorce as well."

I was gone, leaving Grace in awe and shock.

As I drove back to the Inn, Trevor was still asleep. Staring at him, I knew I wanted a life with Trevor, and my parents would now be even more proud of me for standing up for what I believed in--myself and my heart.

To My Readers:

I want to say thank you from the bottom of my heart. Your support of my writing has lifted me up when I was having a bad day. I love writing and I hope that my books make you love reading. Remember to have Faith in yourself even when others don't. Every journey begins with the first step. I hope you all enjoy my books. Please look for future books to Come

Acknowledgments

Patrice Krumm: Thank you from the bottom of my heart, your friendship means the world to me. You truly are One in a Million, and I would not trade you for all the Pink in the World.

To my Kick Ass Street Team: I love you all the pink sparkles in the world.

To my family: Thank you for believing in me

To my amazing Beta readers: Candice Burna Tice, Amy Abendroth, Jenni Crawford, Stephanie Nett, Rhonda Reuther, and all who helped in this journey.

To my Proofreader: Jenni Crawford, may there always be too many commas in all my books. I always add extras just for you.

To all the amazing authors who are part of this boxed set, I am extremely honored to be considered one of you. Thank you for taking a chance with me.

To the love of my life Rhonda Reuther, may our love always endure life's struggles. And may your "issues" always be taken care of. Love you all the red skittles.

To my Mom: Thank you for giving me the love of reading when I was younger. It has inspired me to become who I am today.

And to my amazing Daughter, Thank you for being my number one fan. I love you gumdrops and popsicles.

SC Hutchinson: Thank you for all you do for me. You truly are an amazing friend.

Meet the Author

I was born in Tulsa, Oklahoma but moved to Pensacola, Florida in 1996. I have a huge family who I shocked them when I told them I was writing my first book. I have had a love a reading since I was young. Reading has always been my escape. I can read and be a princess or a warrior. Reading for me was always something magical. And I hope to pass that on to you all.

I am blessed to be the mom of a little girl named Sage who is the light of my life. {I call her Olga, and she hates it} I did not give birth to her but I choose her.

I am blessed with great friends who have always had my back. I have a lot to learn in this world of writing but, so far I am enjoying the ride. I have a fantastic Four that are my true loves. No names will be mentioned as they know who they are. I Love you all very much. {I didn't included alters in that comment}.

I'm very opinionated and have no filter. I speak my mind without thinking of the consequences. Does this get me in Trouble? Yes it does every single day. But I will not change. I March to my own beat. My mom says that I can be a one man band.
I am always willing to help out anyone who is in need all you have to do is ask. I never knew that writing a book would show me so much about myself. I have learned so much in a short amount of time. And I can't wait to learn more.

This past year has truly blessed me in so many ways. I was nominated on several blogs for best LBGT author, and guess what? I won on Coast to Coast Book Besties. Needless to say I'm over the moon excited because I'm firm believer in Equal Rights. So in my books you will find a little bit of everything. I'm not ashamed to step out of the normal cookie cutter box. I like to push the limits, and I love to be different.

"Always remember to let your Faith be bigger than your fear." ~ Layla Stevens

Are you Stalking me? If your answer is no then you should.

Instagram @authorlayla
Pintrest authorlayla
Google + Layla Stevens
Pizap Layla.stevens.author@gmail.com
Tumblir @authorlayla
Twitter @authorlayla
Email Layla.Stevens.author@gmail.com

Like page
https://www.facebook.com/pages/Layla-Stevens/697947530238039

Amazon page
http://www.amazon.com/Layla-Stevens/e/B00MRB0TTM/ref=ntt_athr_dp_pel_1

Buy Links Amazon
Us http://www.amazon.com/dp/B00MR3HQZ0

Goodreads
http://www.goodreads.com/book/show/18773845-broken-love-and-forever-bound

Goodreads Damaged Love
https://www.goodreads.com/book/show/25089097-damaged-love

Goodreads Once Anthology
https://www.goodreads.com/book/show/25439598-once-a-collection-of-sinfully-sexy-and-twisted-tales

Goodreads Love Thyself
https://www.goodreads.com/book/show/26228725-love-thyself?from_search=true&search_version=service

Goodreads Mouth Anthology
https://www.goodreads.com/book/show/26840028-mouth?from_search=true&search_version=service

Goodreads Inspirational Beautiful Eescape 2
https://www.goodreads.com/book/show/25824877-this-beautiful-escape-2?from_search=true&search_version=service

Plague
My new addiction http://plag.com/app/

www.ingramcontent.com/pod-product-compliance
Lightning Source LLC
Chambersburg PA
CBHW070654130626
46555CB00006B/2868